NORWOOD HOUSE  PRESS

Come to the Farm

By Kathleen Corrigan

Search for Sounds
Consonants: c, g

Scan this code to access the Teacher's Notes for this series or visit
www.norwoodhousepress.com/decodables

DEAR CAREGIVER, *The Decodables* series contains books following a systematic, cumulative phonics scope and sequence aligned with the science of reading. Each book in the *Search for Sounds* series allows its reader to apply their phonemic awareness and phonics knowledge in engaging and relatable texts. The keywords within each text have been carefully selected to allow readers to identify pictures beginning with sounds and letters they have been explicitly taught.

When reading these books with your child, encourage them to isolate the beginning sound in the keywords, find the corresponding picture, and identify the letter that makes the beginning sound by pointing to the letter placed in the corner of each page. Rereading the texts multiple times will allow your child the opportunity to build their letter sound fluency, a skill necessary for decoding.

You can be confident you are providing your child with opportunities to build their foundational decoding abilities which will encourage their independence as they become lifelong readers.

Happy Reading!

Emily Nudds, M.S. Ed Literacy
Literacy Consultant

3

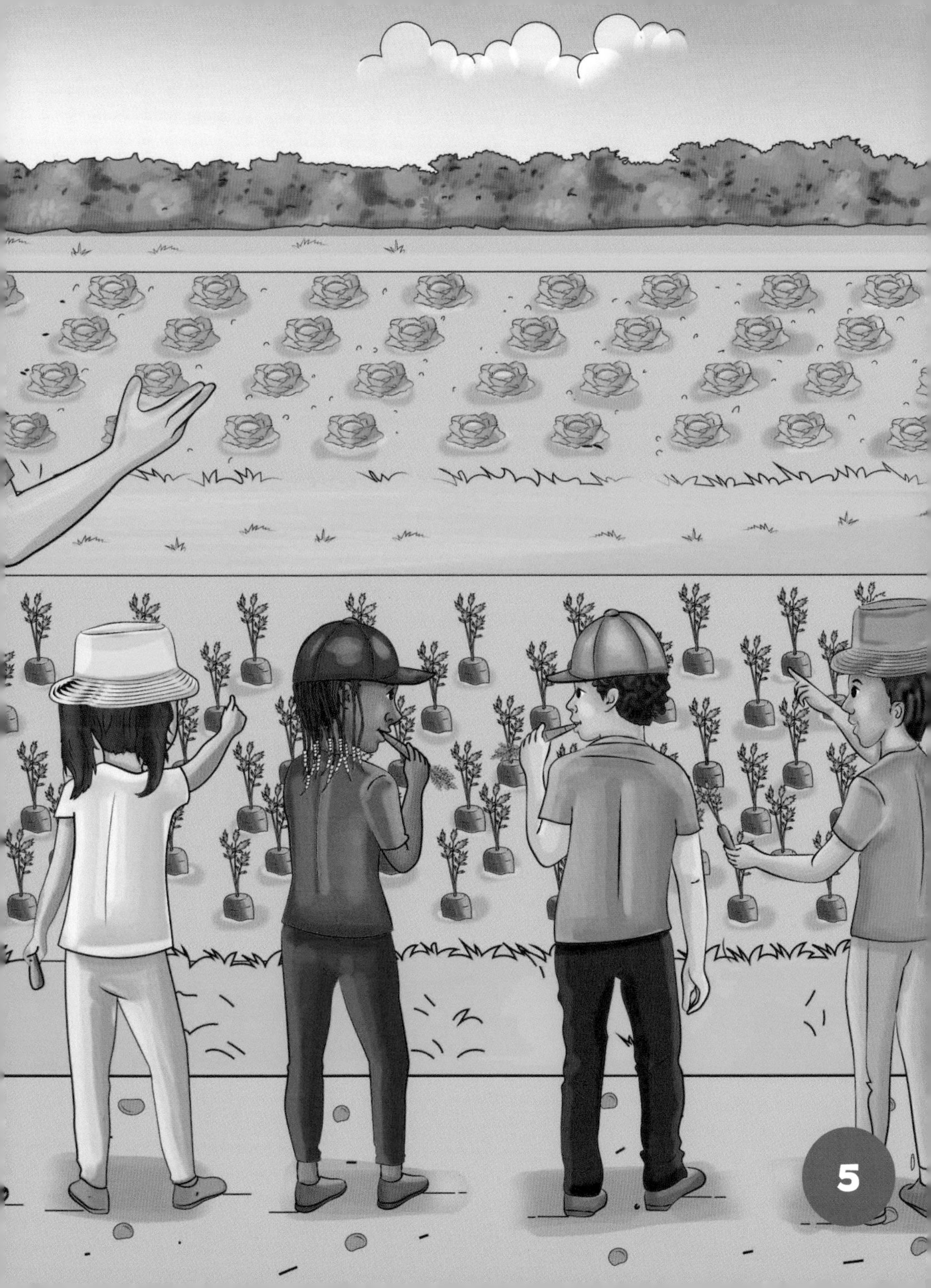

c g

10

HOW TO USE THIS BOOK

Read this text with your child as they engage with each page. Then, read each keyword and ask them to isolate the beginning sound before finding the corresponding picture in the illustration. Encourage finding and pointing to the corresponding letter in the corner of the page. Additional reinforcement activities can be found in the Teacher's Notes.

Come to the Farm
Hard g

Pages 2 and 3	Hi! I am Gale and I am a girl in my kindergarten class. Today we are visiting the farm. I am so excited. We explore the farm in our groups. I am in a group with my friends Zara, Victor, and Bob. Every group has a grownup. Our grownup is Victor's dad, Mr. Grant! He is fun.

First, we are going to see the goats. Mr. Grant says we must be careful when we go through the gate. Some of the goats like to try and escape. They can get into trouble outside their pen. They might run on the road or eat something gross. Did you know that goats will even look in the garbage to see if they can find food they like? |
| Keywords: Gale, girl, goats, (Mr.) Grant, gravel, green, group, grownup | |

Hard c

Pages 4 and 5

The goats were fun, but now we are looking at big fields full of crops. Crops are the plants the farmers grow. They have a lot of crops here. I can see some of my favorites, like corn and cabbage and carrots.

We can see a funny scarecrow in the corn field. The farmer told us the scarecrow scares away crows and other birds that eat their crops. But I see a crow sneaking past the scarecrow! I wonder if it will get some corn.

We each got to pull up a carrot to eat. We had to wash off the dirt, but now it is crunchy and delicious.

Keywords: cabbage, carrot, corn, crops, crow

Read this text with your child as they engage with each page. Then, read each keyword and ask them to isolate the beginning sound before finding the corresponding picture in the illustration. Encourage finding and pointing to the corresponding letter in the corner of the page. Additional reinforcement activities can be found in the Teacher's Notes.

Hard c and g

Pages 6 and 7

While we were eating our carrots, Mr. Grant took our group over to the fence to see the cows. They look big to me, but they just stand there and chew grass.

A big white goose is walking around the cows. The goose is gobbling. It looks and sounds funny. Maybe they are friends.

We kept walking past all the cattle to look at some of the big machines the farmers use. There is a big tractor with a cultivator behind it. A cultivator digs up the soil between the growing crops so that weeds can't grow.

Mr. Grant showed us some grain in a big barrel. He said that grain was being used to feed the horse and her little colt. The colt is cute. He is galloping in the field.

Keywords: carrots, cattle, colt, cows, crops, cultivator, galloping, girl, goose, grain, grass, group

14

Soft c and g

Pages 8 and 9

Mr. Grant took us past a garden that has celery growing in it.

We are sitting down near the celery to wait for our turn to have a ride on a wagon. The wagon is pulled by a giant horse. It is much bigger than the colt.

There are two plastic circles on the ground. Mr. Grant gives us some pictures of animals to put in the circles. If the animal could live on a farm, like a hen or a pig, it goes in the red circle. If the animal could live in a zoo, a circus, or in the wild, like a giraffe or a lion, it goes in the blue circle.

Keywords: celery, centipede, circle, giant, giraffe

c and g review

Pages 10 and 11

The farm is so big and there is so much to see. But we must go back to school soon, so we start to walk back to the bus.

On our way, we walk past a cellar where the farmer keeps some of the crops to eat in the winter.

Then we pass the chicken coop, where lots of chickens and their babies peck at grain on the ground.

We walk towards a gate while the horses and cows graze on soft green grass. Goodbye farm. What a great day!

Keywords: cellar, coop, cows, crops, gate, giant, girl, goose, grain, grass, graze, green, ground

Norwood House Press • www.norwoodhousepress.com
The Decodables ©2024 by Norwood House Press. All Rights Reserved.
Printed in the United States of America.
367N—082023

Library of Congress Cataloging-in-Publication Data has been filed and is available at
catalog.loc.gov

Literacy Consultant: Emily Nudds, M.S.Ed Literacy
Editorial and Production Development and Management: Focus Strategic Communications Inc.
Editors: Christine Gaba, Christi Davis-Martell
Illustration Credit: Mindmax
Covers: Shutterstock, Macrovector

Hardcover ISBN: 978-1-68450-723-8   Paperback ISBN: 978-1-68404-863-2
eBook ISBN: 978-1-68404-922-6